D1689325

DOVER·THRIFT·EDITIONS

# Songs of Innocence and Songs of Experience

## WILLIAM BLAKE

**DOVER PUBLICATIONS, INC.**
*New York*

# DOVER THRIFT EDITIONS
GENERAL EDITOR: STANLEY APPELBAUM
EDITOR OF THIS VOLUME: PHILIP SMITH

Published in Canada by General Publishing Company, Ltd., 30 Lesmill Road, Don Mills, Toronto, Ontario.

Published in the United Kingdom by Constable and Company, Ltd., 3 The Lanchesters, 162–164 Fulham Palace Road, London W6 9ER.

This Dover edition, first published in 1992, contains the texts of *Songs of Innocence*, published by W. Blake, London, 1789, and *Songs of Experience*, published by W. Blake, London, 1794, as published in facsimile by Dover Publications, Inc., in 1971 and 1984. Punctuation has been editorially revised, and alphabetical lists and a new Note added for this edition.

Manufactured in the United States of America
Dover Publications, Inc., 31 East 2nd Street, Mineola, N.Y. 11501

*Library of Congress Cataloging-in-Publication Data*

Blake, William, 1757–1827.
   [Songs of innocence]
   Songs of innocence ; and, Songs of experience / William Blake.
       p.   cm. — (Dover thrift editions)
   ISBN 0-486-27051-3 (pbk.)
   I. Title: Songs of innocence. II. Title: Songs of experience.
III. Series.
[PR4144.S6   1992]
821'.7—dc20                                                           91-26329
                                                                                        CIP

## Note

ALTHOUGH NEGLECTED UNTIL the end of the nineteenth century, the poetry of William Blake (1757–1827) is today ranked among the most brilliant and original of English verse. Like most of Blake's poems, the collections *Songs of Innocence* (1789) and *Songs of Experience* (added to the former in 1794) originally appeared in very small illustrated editions engraved, printed and hand-colored by Blake, who was equally accomplished as a visual artist.* Stylistically and thematically linked works "Shewing the Two Contrary States of the Human Soul," these collections contain conceits central to Blake's highly idiosyncratic worldview and religious beliefs, which exalted childhood as a beatific state of consciousness as they raged against the shackles imposed by poverty and the sexual norms of the day. In addition to Blake's vivid and personal approach to his art, these tenets have proven portentous of many literary and social developments to come, from the English Romantics to the Beat Generation.

---

*Color facsimiles of these original editions are available from Dover Publications: *Songs of Innocence* (0-486-22764-2) and *Songs of Experience* (0-486-24636-1).

# Contents

## SONGS OF INNOCENCE (1789)

| | page |
|---|---|
| Introduction | 3 |
| The Shepherd | 4 |
| Infant Joy | 4 |
| On Another's Sorrow | 5 |
| The School Boy | 6 |
| HOLY THURSDAY | 8 |
| Nurse's Song | 8 |
| Laughing Song | 9 |
| The Little Black Boy | 10 |
| The Voice of the Ancient Bard | 11 |
| The Ecchoing Green | 11 |
| The Chimney Sweeper | 13 |
| The Divine Image | 14 |
| A Dream | 15 |
| The Little Girl Lost | 16 |
| The Little Girl Found | 18 |
| The Little Boy Lost | 20 |
| The Little Boy Found | 21 |
| A CRADLE SONG | 21 |
| Spring | 23 |
| The Blossom | 24 |
| The Lamb | 24 |
| Night | 25 |

## SONGS OF EXPERIENCE (1794)

*page*

| | |
|---|---:|
| Introduction | 31 |
| EARTH'S Answer | 32 |
| The CLOD & the PEBBLE | 33 |
| HOLY THURSDAY | 33 |
| THE Chimney Sweeper | 34 |
| NURSE'S Song | 35 |
| The SICK ROSE | 35 |
| THE FLY | 36 |
| The Angel | 37 |
| The Tyger | 37 |
| My Pretty ROSE TREE | 39 |
| AH! SUN-FLOWER | 39 |
| THE LILLY | 40 |
| The GARDEN of LOVE | 40 |
| The Little Vagabond | 41 |
| LONDON | 41 |
| The Human Abstract | 42 |
| INFANT SORROW | 43 |
| A POISON TREE | 44 |
| A Little BOY Lost | 44 |
| A Little GIRL Lost | 46 |
| To Tirzah | 47 |
| | |
| Alphabetical List of Titles | 49 |
| Alphabetical List of First Lines | 51 |

# Songs of Innocence

## Introduction

Piping down the valleys wild,
Piping songs of pleasant glee,
On a cloud I saw a child,
And he laughing said to me:

"Pipe a song about a Lamb!"
So I piped with merry chear.
"Piper, pipe that song again;"
So I piped, he wept to hear.

"Drop thy pipe, thy happy pipe;
Sing thy songs of happy chear:"
So I sung the same again,
While he wept with joy to hear.

"Piper, sit thee down and write
In a book, that all may read."
So he vanish'd from my sight,
And I pluck'd a hollow reed,

And I made a rural pen,
And I stain'd the water clear,
And I wrote my happy songs
Every child may joy to hear.

### The Shepherd

How sweet is the Shepherd's sweet lot!
From the morn to the evening he strays;
He shall follow his sheep all the day,
And his tongue shall be filled with praise.


For he hears the lamb's innocent call,
And he hears the ewe's tender reply;
He is watchful while they are in peace,
For they know when their Shepherd is nigh.


### Infant Joy

"I have no name:
I am but two days old."
What shall I call thee?
"I happy am,
Joy is my name."
Sweet joy befall thee!

Pretty joy!
Sweet joy, but two days old.
Sweet joy I call thee:
Thou dost smile,
I sing the while,
Sweet joy befall thee!

### On Another's Sorrow

Can I see another's woe,
And not be in sorrow too?
Can I see another's grief,
And not seek for kind relief?

Can I see a falling tear,
And not feel my sorrow's share?
Can a father see his child
Weep, nor be with sorrow fill'd?

Can a mother sit and hear
An infant groan, an infant fear?
No, no! never can it be!
Never, never can it be!

And can he who smiles on all
Hear the wren with sorrows small,
Hear the small bird's grief & care,
Hear the woes that infants bear,

And not sit beside the nest,
Pouring pity in their breast;
And not sit the cradle near,
Weeping tear on infant's tear;

And not sit both night & day,
Wiping all our tears away?

O! no, never can it be!
Never, never can it be!

He doth give his joy to all;
He becomes an infant small;
He becomes a man of woe;
He doth feel the sorrow too.

Think not thou canst sigh a sigh,
And thy maker is not by;
Think not thou canst weep a tear,
And thy maker is not near.

O! he gives to us his joy
That our grief he may destroy;
Till our grief is fled & gone
He doth sit by us and moan.

## The School Boy

I love to rise in a summer morn
When the birds sing on every tree;
The distant huntsman winds his horn,
And the sky-lark sings with me.
O! what sweet company.

But to go to school in a summer morn,
O! it drives all joy away;

Under a cruel eye outworn,
The little ones spend the day
In sighing and dismay.

Ah! then at times I drooping sit,
And spend many an anxious hour,
Nor in my book can I take delight,
Nor sit in learning's bower,
Worn thro' with the dreary shower.

How can the bird that is born for joy
Sit in a cage and sing?
How can a child, when fears annoy,
But droop his tender wing,
And forget his youthful spring?

O! father & mother, if buds are nip'd
And blossoms blown away,
And if the tender plants are strip'd
Of their joy in the springing day,
By sorrow and care's dismay,

How shall the summer arise in joy,
Or the summer fruits appear?
Or how shall we gather what griefs destroy,
Or bless the mellowing year,
When the blasts of winter appear?

## HOLY THURSDAY

'Twas on a Holy Thursday, their innocent faces clean,
The children walking two & two, in red & blue & green,
Grey-headed beadles walk'd before, with wands as white as snow,
Till into the high dome of Paul's they like Thames' waters flow.

O what a multitude they seem'd, these flowers of London town!
Seated in companies they sit with radiance all their own.
The hum of multitudes was there, but multitudes of lambs,
Thousands of little boys & girls raising their innocent hands.

Now like a mighty wind they raise to heaven the voice of song,
Or like harmonious thunderings the seats of heaven among.
Beneath them sit the aged men, wise guardians of the poor;
Then cherish pity, lest you drive an angel from your door.


### Nurse's Song

When the voices of children are heard on the green,
And laughing is heard on the hill,
My heart is at rest within my breast,
And everything else is still.

"Then come home, my children, the sun is gone down,
And the dews of night arise;
Come, come, leave off play, and let us away
Till the morning appears in the skies."

"No, no, let us play, for it is yet day,
And we cannot go to sleep;
Besides, in the sky the little birds fly,
And the hills are all cover'd with sheep."

"Well, well, go & play till the light fades away,
And then go home to bed."
The little ones leaped & shouted & laugh'd
And all the hills ecchoed.

## Laughing Song

When the green woods laugh with the voice of joy,
And the dimpling stream runs laughing by;
When the air does laugh with our merry wit,
And the green hill laughs with the noise of it;

When the meadows laugh with lively green,
And the grasshopper laughs in the merry scene,
When Mary and Susan and Emily
With their sweet round mouths sing "Ha, Ha, He!"

When the painted birds laugh in the shade,
Where our table with cherries and nuts is spread,
Come live & be merry, and join with me,
To sing the sweet chorus of "Ha, Ha, He!"

## The Little Black Boy

My mother bore me in the southern wild,
And I am black, but O! my soul is white;
White as an angel is the English child,
But I am black as if bereav'd of light.

My mother taught me underneath a tree,
And, sitting down before the heat of day,
She took me on her lap and kissed me,
And pointing to the east began to say:

"Look on the rising sun: there God does live,
And gives his light, and gives his heat away;
And flowers and trees and beasts and men recieve
Comfort in morning, joy in the noonday.

"And we are put on earth a little space,
That we may learn to bear the beams of love;
And these black bodies and this sunburnt face
Is but a cloud, and like a shady grove.

"For when our souls have learn'd the heat to bear,
The cloud will vanish; we shall hear his voice,
Saying: 'Come out from the grove, my love & care,
And round my golden tent like lambs rejoice.'"

Thus did my mother say, and kissed me;
And thus I say to little English boy.

When I from black and he from white cloud free,
And round the tent of God like lambs we joy,

I'll shade him from the heat, till he can bear
To lean in joy upon our father's knee;
And then I'll stand and stroke his silver hair,
And be like him, and he will then love me.


### The Voice of the Ancient Bard

Youth of delight, come hither,
And see the opening morn,
Image of truth new-born.
Doubt is fled & clouds of reason,
Dark disputes & artful teazing.
Folly is an endless maze,
Tangled roots perplex her ways.
How many have fallen there!
They stumble all night over bones of the dead,
And feel they know not what but care,
And wish to lead others, when they should be led.


### The Ecchoing Green

The Sun does arise,
And make happy the skies;
The merry bells ring

To welcome the Spring;
The sky-lark and thrush,
The birds of the bush,
Sing louder around
To the bells' chearful sound,
While our sports shall be seen
On the Ecchoing Green.

Old John, with white hair,
Does laugh away care,
Sitting under the oak,
Among the old folk.
They laugh at our play,
And soon they all say:
"Such, such were the joys
When we all, girls & boys,
In our youth time were seen
On the Ecchoing Green."

Till the little ones, weary,
No more can be merry;
The sun does descend,
And our sports have an end.
Round the laps of their mothers
Many sisters and brothers,
Like birds in their nest,
Are ready for rest,
And sport no more seen
On the darkening Green.

### The Chimney Sweeper

When my mother died I was very young,
And my father sold me while yet my tongue
Could scarcely cry " 'weep! 'weep! 'weep! 'weep!"
So your chimneys I sweep & in soot I sleep.

There's little Tom Dacre, who cried when his head,
That curl'd like a lamb's back, was shav'd: so I said
"Hush, Tom! never mind it, for when your head's bare
You know that the soot cannot spoil your white hair."

And so he was quiet & that very night,
As Tom was a-sleeping, he had such a sight!
That thousands of sweepers, Dick, Joe, Ned & Jack,
Were all of them lock'd up in coffins of black.

And by came an Angel who had a bright key,
And he open'd the coffins & set them all free;
Then down a green plain leaping, laughing, they run,
And wash in a river, and shine in the Sun.

Then naked & white, all their bags left behind,
They rise upon clouds and sport in the wind;
And the Angel told Tom, if he'd be a good boy,
He'd have God for his father & never want joy.

And so Tom awoke; and we rose in the dark,
And got with our bags & our brushes to work.

Tho' the morning was cold, Tom was happy & warm;
So if all do their duty they need not fear harm.


### The Divine Image

To Mercy, Pity, Peace, and Love
All pray in their distress;
And to these virtues of delight
Return their thankfulness.

For Mercy, Pity, Peace, and Love
Is God, our father dear,
And Mercy, Pity, Peace, and Love
Is Man, his child and care.

For Mercy has a human heart,
Pity a human face,
And Love, the human form divine,
And Peace, the human dress.

Then every man, of every clime
That prays in his distress,
Prays to the human form divine,
Love, Mercy, Pity, Peace.

And all must love the human form,
In heathen, turk, or jew;
Where Mercy, Love & Pity dwell
There God is dwelling too.

### A Dream

Once a dream did weave a shade
O'er my Angel-guarded bed,
That an Emmet lost its way
Where on grass methought I lay.

Troubled, 'wilder'd, and forlorn,
Dark, benighted, travel-worn,
Over many a tangled spray,
All heart-broke I heard her say:

"O, my children! do they cry?
Do they hear their father sigh?
Now they look abroad to see:
Now return and weep for me."

Pitying, I drop'd a tear;
But I saw a glow-worm near,
Who replied: "What wailing wight
Calls the watchman of the night?

"I am set to light the ground,
While the beetle goes his round:
Follow now the beetle's hum;
Little wanderer, hie thee home."

### The Little Girl Lost

In futurity
I prophetic see
That the earth from sleep
(Grave the sentence deep)

Shall arise and seek
For her maker meek;
And the desart wild
Become a garden mild.

In the southern clime,
Where the summer's prime
Never fades away,
Lovely Lyca lay.

Seven summers old
Lovely Lyca told;
She had wander'd long
Hearing wild birds' song.

"Sweet sleep, come to me
Underneath this tree.
Do father, mother, weep?
Where can Lyca sleep?

"Lost in desart wild
Is your little child.

How can Lyca sleep
If her mother weep?

"If her heart does ake
Then let Lyca wake;
If my mother sleep,
Lyca shall not weep.

"Frowning, frowning night,
O'er this desart bright,
Let thy moon arise
While I close my eyes."

Sleeping Lyca lay
While the beasts of prey,
Come from caverns deep,
View'd the maid asleep.

The kingly lion stood,
And the virgin view'd,
Then he gambol'd round
O'er the hallow'd ground.

Leopards, tygers, play
Round her as she lay,
While the lion old
Bow'd his mane of gold

And her bosom lick,
And upon her neck

From his eyes of flame
Ruby tears there came;

While the lioness
Loos'd her slender dress,
And naked they convey'd
To caves the sleeping maid.

### The Little Girl Found

All the night in woe
Lyca's parents go
Over vallies deep,
While the desarts weep.

Tired and woe-begone,
Hoarse with making moan,
Arm in arm seven days
They trac'd the desert ways.

Seven nights they sleep
Among shadows deep,
And dream they see their child
Starv'd in desert wild.

Pale, thro' pathless ways
The fancied image strays

Famish'd, weeping, weak,
With hollow piteous shriek.

Rising from unrest,
The trembling woman prest
With feet of weary woe:
She could no further go.

In his arms he bore
Her, arm'd with sorrow sore;
Till before their way
A couching lion lay.

Turning back was vain:
Soon his heavy mane
Bore them to the ground.
Then he stalk'd around,

Smelling to his prey;
But their fears allay
When he licks their hands,
And silent by them stands.

They look upon his eyes
Fill'd with deep surprise;
And wondering behold
A Spirit arm'd in gold.

On his head a crown;
On his shoulders down

Flow'd his golden hair.
Gone was all their care.

"Follow me," he said;
"Weep not for the maid;
In my palace deep
Lyca lies asleep."

Then they followed
Where the vision led,
And saw their sleeping child
Among tygers wild.

To this day they dwell
In a lonely dell;
Nor fear the wolvish howl
Nor the lions' growl.

### The Little Boy Lost

"Father! father! where are you going?
O do not walk so fast.
Speak, father, speak to your little boy,
Or else I shall be lost."

The night was dark, no father was there;
The child was wet with dew;
The mire was deep, & the child did weep,
And away the vapour flew.

### The Little Boy Found

The little boy lost in the lonely fen,
Led by the wand'ring light,
Began to cry; but God, ever nigh,
Appear'd like his father, in white.

He kissed the child, & by the hand led,
And to his mother brought,
Who in sorrow pale, thro' the lonely dale,
Her little boy weeping sought.

### A CRADLE SONG

Sweet dreams form a shade
O'er my lovely infant's head;
Sweet dreams of pleasant streams
By happy, silent, moony beams.

Sweet sleep with soft down
Weave thy brows an infant crown.
Sweet sleep, Angel mild,
Hover o'er my happy child.

Sweet smiles in the night
Hover over my delight;
Sweet smiles, Mother's smiles,
All the livelong night beguiles.

Sweet moans, dovelike sighs,
Chase not slumber from thy eyes.
Sweet moans, sweeter smiles,
All the dovelike moans beguiles.

Sleep sleep, happy child,
All creation slept and smil'd;
Sleep sleep, happy sleep,
While o'er thee thy mother weep.

Sweet babe, in thy face
Holy image I can trace.
Sweet babe, once like thee,
Thy maker lay and wept for me,

Wept for me, for thee, for all,
When he was an infant small.
Thou his image ever see,
Heavenly face that smiles on thee,

Smiles on thee, on me, on all;
Who became an infant small.
Infant smiles are his own smiles;
Heaven & earth to peace beguiles.

## Spring

Sound the Flute!
Now it's mute.
Birds delight
Day and Night;
Nightingale
In the dale,
Lark in Sky,
Merrily,
Merrily, Merrily, to welcome in the Year.

Little Boy,
Full of joy;
Little Girl,
Sweet and small;
Cock does crow,
So do you;
Merry voice,
Infant noise,
Merrily, Merrily, to welcome in the Year.

Little Lamb,
Here I am;
Come and lick
My white neck;
Let me pull
Your soft Wool;

Let me kiss
Your soft face:
Merrily, Merrily, we welcome in the Year.

## The Blossom

Merry Merry Sparrow!
Under leaves so green,
A happy Blossom
Sees you, swift as arrow,
Seek your cradle narrow
Near my Bosom.

Pretty Pretty Robin!
Under leaves so green,
A happy Blossom
Hears you sobbing, sobbing,
Pretty Pretty Robin,
Near my Bosom.

## The Lamb

Little Lamb, who made thee?
  Dost thou know who made thee?
Gave thee life & bid thee feed,
By the stream & o'er the mead;
Gave thee clothing of delight,
Softest clothing, wooly, bright;

Gave thee such a tender voice,
Making all the vales rejoice?
   Little Lamb, who made thee?
   Dost thou know who made thee?

   Little Lamb, I'll tell thee,
   Little Lamb, I'll tell thee:
He is called by thy name,
For he calls himself a Lamb.
He is meek & he is mild;
He became a little child.
I a child & thou a lamb.
We are called by his name.
   Little Lamb, God bless thee!
   Little Lamb, God bless thee!

## Night

The sun descending in the west,
The evening star does shine;
The birds are silent in their nest,
And I must seek for mine.
The moon like a flower,
In heaven's high bower,
With silent delight
Sits and smiles on the night.

Farewell, green fields and happy groves,
Where flocks have took delight;

Where lambs have nibbled, silent moves
The feet of angels bright;
Unseen they pour blessing,
And joy without ceasing,
On each bud and blossom,
And each sleeping bosom.

They look in every thoughtless nest,
Where birds are cover'd warm;
They visit caves of every beast,
To keep them all from harm;
If they see any weeping
That should have been sleeping,
They pour sleep on their head
And sit down by their bed.

When wolves and tygers howl for prey,
They pitying stand and weep;
Seeking to drive their thirst away,
And keep them from the sheep.
But if they rush dreadful,
The angels, most heedful,
Recieve each mild spirit,
New worlds to inherit.

And there the lion's ruddy eyes
Shall flow with tears of gold,
And pitying the tender cries,
And walking round the fold,

Saying "Wrath, by his meekness,
And, by his health, sickness
Is driven away
From our immortal day.

"And now beside thee, bleating lamb,
I can lie down and sleep;
Or think on him who bore thy name,
Graze after thee and weep.
For, wash'd in life's river,
My bright mane for ever
Shall shine like the gold
As I guard o'er the fold."

# Songs of Experience

## Introduction

Hear the voice of the Bard!
Who Present, Past, & Future, sees;
Whose ears have heard
The Holy Word
That walk'd among the ancient trees,

Calling the lapsed Soul,
And weeping in the evening dew;
That might controll
The starry pole,
And fallen, fallen light renew!

"O Earth, O Earth, return!
"Arise from out the dewy grass;
"Night is worn,
"And the morn
"Rises from the slumberous mass.

"Turn away no more;
"Why wilt thou turn away?
"The starry floor,
"The wat'ry shore,
"Is giv'n thee till the break of day."

### EARTH'S Answer

Earth rais'd up her head
From the darkness dread & drear.
Her light fled,
Stony dread!
And her locks cover'd with grey despair.

"Prison'd on wat'ry shore,
"Starry Jealousy does keep my den:
"Cold and hoar,
"Weeping o'er,
"I hear the Father of the ancient men.

"Selfish father of men!
"Cruel, jealous, selfish fear!
"Can delight,
"Chain'd in night,
"The virgins of youth and morning bear?

"Does spring hide its joy
"When buds and blossoms grow?
"Does the sower
"Sow by night,
"Or the plowman in darkness plow?

"Break this heavy chain
"That does freeze my bones around.

"Selfish! vain!
"Eternal bane!
"That free Love with bondage bound."


### The CLOD & the PEBBLE

"Love seeketh not Itself to please,
"Nor for itself hath any care,
"But for another gives its ease,
"And builds a Heaven in Hell's despair."


So sang a little Clod of Clay
Trodden with the cattle's feet,
But a Pebble of the brook
Warbled out these metres meet:


"Love seeketh only Self to please,
"To bind another to Its delight,
"Joys in another's loss of ease,
"And builds a Hell in Heaven's despite."


### HOLY THURSDAY

Is this a holy thing to see
In a rich and fruitful land,
Babes reduc'd to misery,
Fed with cold and usurous hand?

Is that trembling cry a song?
Can it be a song of joy?
And so many children poor?
It is a land of poverty!

And their sun does never shine,
And their fields are bleak & bare,
And their ways are fill'd with thorns:
It is eternal winter there.

For where-e'er the sun does shine,
And where-e'er the rain does fall,
Babe can never hunger there,
Nor poverty the mind appall.

## THE Chimney Sweeper

A little black thing among the snow,
Crying ' 'weep! 'weep!' in notes of woe!
"Where are thy father & mother? say?"
"They are both gone up to the church to pray.

"Because I was happy upon the heath,
"And smil'd among the winter's snow,
"They clothed me in the clothes of death,
"And taught me to sing the notes of woe.

"And because I am happy & dance & sing,
"They think they have done me no injury,

"And are gone to praise God & his Priest & King,
"Who make up a heaven of our misery."


### NURSE'S Song

When the voices of children are heard on the green
And whisp'rings are in the dale,
The days of my youth rise fresh in my mind,
My face turns green and pale.

Then come home, my children, the sun is gone down,
And the dews of night arise;
Your spring & your day are wasted in play,
And your winter and night in disguise.


### The SICK ROSE

O Rose, thou art sick!
The invisible worm
That flies in the night,
In the howling storm,

Has found out thy bed
Of crimson joy:
And his dark secret love
Does thy life destroy.

## THE FLY

Little Fly,
Thy summer's play
My thoughtless hand
Has brush'd away.

Am not I
A fly like thee?
Or art not thou
A man like me?

For I dance,
And drink, & sing,
Till some blind hand
Shall brush my wing.

If thought is life
And strength & breath,
And the want
Of thought is death;

Then am I
A happy fly,
If I live
Or if I die.

## The Angel

I Dreamt a Dream! what can it mean?
And that I was a maiden Queen,
Guarded by an Angel mild:
Witless woe was ne'er beguil'd!

And I wept both night and day,
And he wip'd my tears away,
And I wept both day and night,
And hid from him my heart's delight.

So he took his wings and fled;
Then the morn blush'd rosy red;
I dried my tears, & arm'd my fears
With ten thousand shields and spears.

Soon my Angel came again:
I was arm'd, he came in vain;
For the time of youth was fled,
And grey hairs were on my head.

## The Tyger

Tyger! Tyger! burning bright
In the forests of the night,
What immortal hand or eye
Could frame thy fearful symmetry?

In what distant deeps or skies
Burnt the fire of thine eyes?
On what wings dare he aspire?
What the hand dare sieze the fire?

And what shoulder, & what art,
Could twist the sinews of thy heart?
And when thy heart began to beat,
What dread hand? & what dread feet?

What the hammer? what the chain?
In what furnace was thy brain?
What the anvil? what dread grasp
Dare its deadly terrors clasp?

When the stars threw down their spears,
And water'd heaven with their tears,
Did he smile his work to see?
Did he who made the Lamb make thee?

Tyger! Tyger! burning bright
In the forests of the night,
What immortal hand or eye
Dare frame thy fearful symmetry?

## My Pretty ROSE TREE

A flower was offer'd to me,
Such a flower as May never bore;
But I said "I've a Pretty Rose-tree,"
And I passed the sweet flower o'er.

Then I went to my Pretty Rose-tree,
To tend her by day and by night;
But my Rose turn'd away with jealousy,
And her thorns were my only delight.

## AH! SUN-FLOWER

Ah, Sun-flower, weary of time,
Who countest the steps of the Sun,
Seeking after that sweet golden clime
Where the traveller's journey is done:

Where the Youth pined away with desire,
And the pale Virgin shrouded in snow
Arise from their graves, and aspire
Where my Sun-flower wishes to go.

## THE LILLY

The modest Rose puts forth a thorn,
The humble Sheep a threat'ning horn;
While the Lilly white shall in Love delight,
Nor a thorn, nor a threat, stain her beauty bright.


### The GARDEN of LOVE

I went to the Garden of Love,
And saw what I never had seen:
A Chapel was built in the midst,
Where I used to play on the green.

And the gates of this Chapel were shut,
And "Thou shalt not" writ over the door;
So I turn'd to the Garden of Love
That so many sweet flowers bore;

And I saw it was filled with graves,
And tomb-stones where flowers should be;
And Priests in black gowns were walking their rounds,
And binding with briars my joys & desires.

### The Little Vagabond

Dear Mother, dear Mother, the Church is cold,
But the Ale-house is healthy & pleasant & warm;
Besides I can tell where I am used well,
Such usage in heaven will never do well.

But if at the Church they would give us some Ale,
And a pleasant fire our souls to regale,
We'd sing and we'd pray all the live-long day,
Nor ever once wish from the Church to stray.

Then the Parson might preach, & drink, & sing,
And we'd be as happy as birds in the spring;
And modest dame Lurch, who is always at Church,
Would not have bandy children, nor fasting, nor birch.

And God, like a father rejoicing to see
His children as pleasant and happy as he,
Would have no more quarrel with the Devil or the Barrel,
But kiss him, & give him both drink and apparel.

### LONDON

I wander thro' each charter'd street,
Near where the charter'd Thames does flow,
And mark in every face I meet
Marks of weakness, marks of woe.

In every cry of every Man,
In every Infant's cry of fear,
In every voice, in every ban,
The mind-forg'd manacles I hear.

How the Chimney-sweeper's cry
Every black'ning Church appalls;
And the hapless Soldier's sigh
Runs in blood down Palace walls.

But most thro' midnight streets I hear
How the youthful Harlot's curse
Blasts the new born Infant's tear,
And blights with plagues the Marriage hearse.

## The Human Abstract

Pity would be no more
If we did not make somebody Poor;
And Mercy no more could be
If all were as happy as we.

And mutual fear brings peace,
Till the selfish loves increase:
Then Cruelty knits a snare,
And spreads his baits with care.

He sits down with holy fears,
And waters the ground with tears;

Then Humility takes its root
Underneath his foot.

Soon spreads the dismal shade
Of Mystery over his head;
And the Catterpiller and Fly
Feed on the Mystery.

And it bears the fruit of Deceit,
Ruddy and sweet to eat;
And the Raven his nest has made
In its thickest shade.

The Gods of the earth and sea
Sought thro' Nature to find this Tree;
But their search was all in vain:
There grows one in the Human Brain.

## INFANT SORROW

My mother groan'd! my father wept.
Into the dangerous world I leapt:
Helpless, naked, piping loud:
Like a fiend hid in a cloud.

Struggling in my father's hands,
Striving against my swadling bands,
Bound and weary I thought best
To sulk upon my mother's breast.

## A POISON TREE

I was angry with my friend:
I told my wrath, my wrath did end.
I was angry with my foe:
I told it not, my wrath did grow.

And I water'd it in fears,
Night & morning with my tears;
And I sunned it with smiles,
And with soft deceitful wiles.

And it grew both day and night,
Till it bore an apple bright;
And my foe beheld it shine,
And he knew that it was mine,

And into my garden stole
When the night had veil'd the pole:
In the morning glad I see
My foe outstretch'd beneath the tree.

## A Little BOY Lost

"Nought loves another as itself,
"Nor venerates another so,
"Nor is it possible to Thought
"A greater than itself to know:

"And Father, how can I love you
"Or any of my brothers more?
"I love you like the little bird
"That picks up crumbs around the door."

The Priest sat by and heard the child,
In trembling zeal he siez'd his hair:
He led him by his little coat,
And all admir'd the Priestly care.

And standing on the altar high,
"Lo! what a fiend is here!" said he,
"One who sets reason up for judge
"Of our most holy Mystery."

The weeping child could not be heard,
The weeping parents wept in vain;
They strip'd him to his little shirt,
And bound him in an iron chain;

And burn'd him in a holy place,
Where many had been burn'd before:
The weeping parents wept in vain.
Are such things done on Albion's shore?

### A Little GIRL Lost

*Children of the future Age*
*Reading this indignant page,*
*Know that in a former time*
*Love! sweet Love! was thought a crime.*


In the Age of Gold,
Free from winter's cold,
Youth and maiden bright
To the holy light,
Naked in the sunny beams delight.


Once a youthful pair,
Fill'd with softest care,
Met in garden bright
Where the holy light
Had just remov'd the curtains of the night.


There, in rising day
On the grass they play;
Parents were afar,
Strangers came not near,
And the maiden soon forgot her fear.


Tired with kisses sweet,
They agree to meet
When the silent sleep

Waves o'er heaven's deep,
And the weary tired wanderers weep.

To her father white
Came the maiden bright;
But his loving look,
Like the holy book,
All her tender limbs with terror shook.

"Ona! pale and weak!
"To thy father speak:
"O, the trembling fear!
"O, the dismal care!
"That shakes the blossoms of my hoary hair."


### To Tirzah

*[Probably added about 1801]*

Whate'er is Born of Mortal Birth
Must be consumed with the Earth
To rise from Generation free:
Then what have I to do with thee?

The Sexes sprung from Shame & Pride,
Blow'd in the morn; in evening died;
But Mercy chang'd Death into Sleep;
The Sexes rose to work & weep.

Thou, Mother of my Mortal part,
With cruelty didst mould my Heart,
And with false self-decieving tears
Didst bind my Nostrils, Eyes, & Ears:

Didst close my Tongue in senseless clay,
And me to Mortal Life betray.
The Death of Jesus set me free:
Then what have I to do with thee?

## Alphabetical List of Titles

|  | page |
|---|---|
| AH! SUN-FLOWER | 39 |
| Angel, The | 37 |
| Blossom, The | 24 |
| Chimney Sweeper, The | 13 |
| Chimney Sweeper, THE | 34 |
| CLOD & the PEBBLE, The | 33 |
| CRADLE SONG, A | 21 |
| Divine Image, The | 14 |
| Dream, A | 15 |
| EARTH'S Answer | 32 |
| Ecchoing Green, The | 11 |
| FLY, THE | 36 |
| GARDEN of LOVE, The | 40 |
| HOLY THURSDAY | 8 |
| HOLY THURSDAY | 33 |
| Human Abstract, The | 42 |
| Infant Joy | 4 |
| INFANT SORROW | 43 |
| Introduction [Songs of Experience] | 31 |

|  | page |
|---|---|
| Introduction [*Songs of Innocence*] | 3 |
| Lamb, The | 24 |
| Laughing Song | 9 |
| LILLY, THE | 40 |
| Little Black Boy, The | 10 |
| Little Boy Found, The | 21 |
| Little BOY Lost, A | 44 |
| Little Boy Lost, The | 20 |
| Little Girl Found, The | 18 |
| Little GIRL Lost, A | 46 |
| Little Girl Lost, The | 16 |
| Little Vagabond, The | 41 |
| LONDON | 41 |
| My Pretty ROSE TREE | 39 |
| Night | 25 |
| Nurse's Song | 8 |
| NURSE'S Song | 35 |
| On Another's Sorrow | 5 |
| POISON TREE, A | 44 |
| School Boy, The | 6 |
| Shepherd, The | 4 |
| SICK ROSE, The | 35 |
| Spring | 23 |
| To Tirzah | 47 |
| Tyger, The | 37 |
| Voice of the Ancient Bard, The | 11 |

# Alphabetical List of First Lines

|  | page |
|---|---|
| A flower was offer'd to me | 39 |
| Ah, Sun-flower, weary of time | 39 |
| A little black thing among the snow | 34 |
| All the night in woe | 18 |
| Can I see another's woe | 5 |
| *Children of the future Age* | 46 |
| Dear Mother, dear Mother, the Church is cold | 41 |
| Earth rais'd up her head | 32 |
| "Father! Father! where are you going?" | 20 |
| Hear the voice of the Bard! | 31 |
| How sweet is the Shepherd's sweet lot! | 4 |
| I Dreamt a Dream! what can it mean? | 37 |
| "I have no name" | 4 |
| I love to rise in a summer morn | 6 |
| In futurity | 16 |
| Is this a holy thing to see | 33 |
| I wander thro' each charter'd street | 41 |
| I was angry with my friend | 44 |

|  | page |
|---|---|
| I went to the Garden of Love | 40 |
| Little Fly | 36 |
| Little Lamb, who made thee? | 24 |
| "Love seeketh not Itself to please" | 33 |
| Merry Merry Sparrow! | 24 |
| My mother bore me in the southern wild | 10 |
| My mother groan'd! my father wept | 43 |
| "Nought loves another as itself" | 44 |
| Once a dream did weave a shade | 15 |
| O Rose, thou art sick! | 35 |
| Piping down the valleys wild | 3 |
| Pity would be no more | 42 |
| Sound the Flute! | 23 |
| Sweet dreams form a shade | 21 |
| The little boy lost in the lonely fen | 21 |
| The modest Rose puts forth a thorn | 40 |
| The sun descending in the west | 25 |
| The Sun does arise | 11 |
| To Mercy, Pity, Peace, and Love | 14 |
| 'Twas on a Holy Thursday, their innocent faces clean | 8 |
| Tyger! Tyger! burning bright | 37 |
| Whate'er is Born of Mortal Birth | 47 |
| When my mother died I was very young | 13 |
| When the green woods laugh with the voice of joy | 9 |
| When the voices of children are heard on the green | 8 |
| When the voices of children are heard on the green | 35 |
| Youth of delight, come hither | 11 |

# DOVER · THRIFT · EDITIONS

All books complete and unabridged. All 5 3/16" × 8 1/4", paperbound.
Just $1.00–$2.00 in U.S.A.

## POETRY (continued)

GREAT LOVE POEMS, Shane Weller (ed.). 128pp. 27284-2 $1.00
SELECTED POEMS, Walt Whitman. 128pp. 26878-0 $1.00
THE BALLAD OF READING GAOL AND OTHER POEMS, Oscar Wilde. 64pp. 27072-6 $1.00
FAVORITE POEMS, William Wordsworth. 80pp. 27073-4 $1.00
EARLY POEMS, William Butler Yeats. 128pp. 27808-5 $1.00

## FICTION

FLATLAND: A ROMANCE OF MANY DIMENSIONS, Edwin A. Abbott. 96pp. 27263-X $1.00
BEOWULF, Beowulf (trans. by R. K. Gordon). 64pp. 27264-8 $1.00
CIVIL WAR STORIES, Ambrose Bierce. 128pp. 28038-1 $1.00
ALICE'S ADVENTURES IN WONDERLAND, Lewis Carroll. 96pp. 27543-4 $1.00
O PIONEERS!, Willa Cather. 128pp. 27785-2 $1.00
FIVE GREAT SHORT STORIES, Anton Chekhov. 96pp. 26463-7 $1.00
FAVORITE FATHER BROWN STORIES, G. K. Chesterton. 96pp. 27545-0 $1.00
THE AWAKENING, Kate Chopin. 128pp. 27786-0 $1.00
HEART OF DARKNESS, Joseph Conrad. 80pp. 26464-5 $1.00
THE SECRET SHARER AND OTHER STORIES, Joseph Conrad. 128pp. 27546-9 $1.00
THE OPEN BOAT AND OTHER STORIES, Stephen Crane. 128pp. 27547-7 $1.00
THE RED BADGE OF COURAGE, Stephen Crane. 112pp. 26465-3 $1.00
A CHRISTMAS CAROL, Charles Dickens. 80pp. 26865-9 $1.00
THE CRICKET ON THE HEARTH AND OTHER CHRISTMAS STORIES, Charles Dickens. 128pp. 28039-X $1.00
NOTES FROM THE UNDERGROUND, Fyodor Dostoyevsky. 96pp. 27053-X $1.00
SIX GREAT SHERLOCK HOLMES STORIES, Sir Arthur Conan Doyle. 112pp. 27055-6 $1.00
WHERE ANGELS FEAR TO TREAD, E. M. Forster. 128pp. (Available in U.S. only) 27791-7 $1.00
THE OVERCOAT AND OTHER SHORT STORIES, Nikolai Gogol. 112pp. 27057-2 $1.00
GREAT GHOST STORIES, John Grafton (ed.). 112pp. 27270-2 $1.00
THE LUCK OF ROARING CAMP AND OTHER SHORT STORIES, Bret Harte. 96pp. 27271-0 $1.00
THE SCARLET LETTER, Nathaniel Hawthorne. 192pp. 28048-9 $2.00
YOUNG GOODMAN BROWN AND OTHER SHORT STORIES, Nathaniel Hawthorne. 128pp. 27060-2 $1.00
THE GIFT OF THE MAGI AND OTHER SHORT STORIES, O. Henry. 96pp. 27061-0 $1.00
THE NUTCRACKER AND THE GOLDEN POT, E. T. A. Hoffmann. 128pp. 27806-9 $1.00
THE BEAST IN THE JUNGLE AND OTHER STORIES, Henry James. 128pp. 27552-3 $1.00
THE TURN OF THE SCREW, Henry James. 96pp. 26684-2 $1.00
DUBLINERS, James Joyce. 160pp. 26870-5 $1.00
A PORTRAIT OF THE ARTIST AS A YOUNG MAN, James Joyce. 192pp. 28050-0 $2.00

# DOVER · THRIFT · EDITIONS

All books complete and unabridged. All 5³⁄₁₆″ × 8¼″, paperbound. Just $1.00–$2.00 in U.S.A.

## FICTION (continued)

The Man Who Would Be King and Other Stories, Rudyard Kipling. 128pp. 28051-9 $1.00

Selected Short Stories, D. H. Lawrence. 128pp. 27794-1 $1.00

Green Tea and Other Ghost Stories, J. Sheridan LeFanu. 96pp. 27795-X $1.00

The Call of the Wild, Jack London. 64pp. 26472-6 $1.00

Five Great Short Stories, Jack London. 96pp. 27063-7 $1.00

White Fang, Jack London. 160pp. 26968-X $1.00

The Necklace and Other Short Stories, Guy de Maupassant. 128pp. 27064-5 $1.00

Bartleby and Benito Cereno, Herman Melville. 112pp. 26473-4 $1.00

The Gold-Bug and Other Tales, Edgar Allan Poe. 128pp. 26875-6 $1.00

The Queen of Spades and Other Stories, Alexander Pushkin. 128pp. 28054-3 $1.00

Three Lives, Gertrude Stein. 176pp. 28059-4 $2.00

The Strange Case of Dr. Jekyll and Mr. Hyde, Robert Louis Stevenson. 64pp. 26688-5 $1.00

Treasure Island, Robert Louis Stevenson. 160pp. 27559-0 $1.00

The Kreutzer Sonata and Other Short Stories, Leo Tolstoy. 144pp. 27805-0 $1.00

Adventures of Huckleberry Finn, Mark Twain. 224pp. 28061-6 $2.00

The Mysterious Stranger and Other Stories, Mark Twain. 128pp. 27069-6 $1.00

Candide, Voltaire (François-Marie Arouet). 112pp. 26689-3 $1.00

The Invisible Man, H. G. Wells. 112pp. (Available in U.S. only.) 27071-8 $1.00

Ethan Frome, Edith Wharton. 96pp. 26690-7 $1.00

The Picture of Dorian Gray, Oscar Wilde. 192pp. 27807-7 $1.00

## NONFICTION

The Devil's Dictionary, Ambrose Bierce. 144pp. 27542-6 $1.00

The Souls of Black Folk, W. E. B. Du Bois. 176pp. 28041-1 $2.00

Self-Reliance and Other Essays, Ralph Waldo Emerson. 128pp. 27790-9 $1.00

Great Speeches, Abraham Lincoln. 112pp. 26872-1 $1.00

The Prince, Niccolò Machiavelli. 80pp. 27274-5 $1.00

Symposium and Phaedrus, Plato. 96pp. 27798-4 $1.00

The Trial and Death of Socrates: Four Dialogues, Plato. 128pp. 27066-1 $1.00

Civil Disobedience and Other Essays, Henry David Thoreau. 96pp. 27563-9 $1.00

The Theory of the Leisure Class, Thorstein Veblen. 256pp. 28062-4 $2.00

## PLAYS

The Cherry Orchard, Anton Chekhov. 64pp. 26682-6 $1.00

The Three Sisters, Anton Chekhov. 64pp. 27544-2 $1.00

The Way of the World, William Congreve. 80pp. 27787-9 $1.00

Medea, Euripides. 64pp. 27548-5 $1.00

The Mikado, William Schwenck Gilbert. 64pp. 27268-0 $1.00